Rain, Rain, Go Away!

To Abril and Emma . . . they are my sunshine on rainy days.

—V.G.

ISBN 978-0-545-46363-8

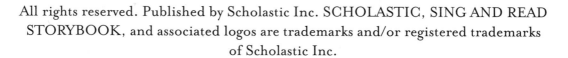
12 11 10 9 8 7 6 5 4 3 2 1   13 14 15 16 17 18/0

Printed in the U.S.A.   40
First printing, April 2013

Book design by Janet Kusmierski

Rain, Rain, Go Away!

Illustrated by Viviana Garofoli

SCHOLASTIC INC.

Rain, rain, go away.
Come again another day.

The boys and girls want to play.
Rain, rain, go away!

Rain, rain, go away!
Come again one April day.

Then flowers will bloom in the month of May.
Rain, rain, go away!

Rain, rain, go away!
Come again on Saturday.

The animals are here, hooray!
Rain, rain, go away!

Rain, rain, go away.
Now the sun would like to stay.

Let everyone come out today.
Rain, rain, go away!

The rain, rain has gone away.

Now sunshine's here to brighten our day.

Rain, Rain, Go Away!

Rain, rain, go a - way.

Come a - gain some an - other day.

The boys and girls want to play.

Rain, rain, go a - way.